For Kall

WITH BEST WISHES

WHERE I SLEEP

From

6-11+ Yrs

*Martin
Author
Feb '24*

Martin Green

Apollo/2020

Copyright © 2020 Martin Green

All rights reserved

The characters and events portrayed in this book are fictitious. Any similarity to real persons, living or dead, is coincidental and not intended by the author.

No part of this book may be reproduced, or stored in a retrieval system, or transmitted in any form or by any means, electronic, mechanical, photocopying, recording, or otherwise, without express written permission of the publisher.

ISBN: 9798647024220

Cover design by: M Green
Library of Congress Control Number: 2018675309

CONTENTS

Title Page	1
Copyright	2
Introduction	5
1- on a Space Station	7
2 – A Flying Boat	12
3 – In a Tent	16
4 – Old Sailing Ship	21
5 – In a Castle (4 Poster Bed)	26
6 – On A Train	31
7 – In a Camper Van	35
8 – On a Cruse Ship	39
9 – In A Log Cabin	43
10 - Moon Base	47
11 – A Passenger Airliner	51
12 - A Big Hotel	55

INTRODUCTION

Sometimes children have trouble getting to sleep, just ask any parent. The good news is that there are ways to help them. One reason they may have trouble getting to sleep can be that their minds are just too busy. Perhaps they are thinking about the things they did during the day, or plan to do the following day. This book contains a series of stories to read to the child at bed time, each leading up to going to sleep. The idea is that you simply redirect their thoughts towards sleeping, and in different and interesting places. Places that they can imagine they are in.

There are twelve different stories, each set in a different and intersting place. Each should take ten or so minutes to read. You should start once the child is in bed and comfortable. Each story leads up to bed time, and ends with a script to relax the child. The script is based in hypnotherapy, but is very mild and in no way hypnotises the child. It simply uses key words like 'relax' and 'restful' to help the child fall asleep. In this book there are several different stories, but you may think of others. You might ask your child where they would like to sleep? It can be somewhere real, somewhere they were happy or somewhere straight from their own imagination. It just has to be a place they would like to be, somewhere they feel safe.

If you find a story they like, repeat it. Sometimes repeating a story can reinforce the effect. Possibly you will hear the child say 'tonight I will sleep on a ship at sea' or 'In space'. Remember, there is nothing very clever or complicated here. Just some short stories to read to the child, helping them imagine they are somewhere else. Somewhere interesting, relaxing and restful.

The script at the end of each story is the same. It can however be varied, it could be read twice. You may think some words would be better for older children then yours? If so, skip them, vary them, put your own in. Think of the script as a guide. Dont expect the child to fall asleep as you read or right at the end, though that might be nice. The idea is simply to get thier minds, and thier wonderful imagination going in the right direction, towards a good nights sleep.

1- ON A SPACE STATION

The space station is high up above the earth. It orbits the planet out in space, going around very quickly. When you're on the space station you don't feel the speed. It's a little like being in a train, you sit and watch the world go by, feeling as if you're almost sitting still. The space station is actually moving so quickly, it circles the entire earth sixteen times for every one turn of the planet. That's one day and night to us. Tonight, we will be sleeping on the space station.

We are now up high above the Earth, we are in space and safely inside a space station. Up here there is no gravity, if you let go of your toothbrush it won't fall down, it will just float there in front of you. It floats in the same way you do in space. It has been a busy day with lots to do. One thing about space stations is that they are not very big, really a series of rooms joined together. Also, without gravity anything not tied down or put away in draws or cupboards just floats around. Being clean and tidy is a good idea anywhere, but never more so than in space.

Everything here has a place to be kept, so anyone on the space station will know where to find it. I often thought it would be better if we tidied our rooms down on earth as if there were no gravity here. It would certainly mean everyone putting things away neatly when finished with them. If we didn't, they would just float off. The day began with a clean and tidy, which included vacuuming. A vacuum cleaner is just as important in space as it is on earth. Dust and small bits and pieces can't be allowed to just float around, they may find their way into important instruments, scientific experiments or controls.

After the clean and tidy, it's off to work. No going to work up here by train or in a car, work is just one or two rooms away. Scientific experiments are what we do up here. Many using the lack of gravity to do things we couldn't do on earth, and others studying the far-off stars and planets. They even study the Earth, learning about the weather and more. Once the day ends its time for a rest, and having something to eat.

The evening meal was nice and very tasty, but you had to take care not to let any of it go while you were holding it. If you did, off it would float. You ate special food, made into bars or inside tubes because a normal plate of food would be no use here. Imagine trying to eat peas on a plate in space? They would get everywhere and tidying them up would take hours.

You finished your food and have brushed your teeth. It's the end of the day and you're tired, very tired and relaxed. You are looking forward to a good sleep. Getting ready for bed in space is like climbing into a sleeping bag when going camping. Only this sleeping bag is attached to the wall to keep it in place. The bag is in your own little room. Not as big as a bedroom on earth, but it's very comfortable. As you climb in and start to close the sleeping bag you think how glad you are to be there.

Being in space is such an adventure. It's been a long day and you have been doing many interesting things. Just before bed, you had also helped fix a radio system, making sure anyone who wanted to could talk to those down on the Earth. You have to be careful when calling home, careful to check what the time is down there.

You're inside the bed now, you closed it up and are very warm and comfy. Next, you switch off the light with the little switch by your side. It goes dark, but if you turn your head a little you can still see some of the small lights spread about the space station. Some are blinking and letting everyone know they are working, and all is well. You can also see a round window from where you sleep. You take a long look, you can see the earth below all blue and white with swirly thick, white clouds. You watch for a few minutes, and see the dark night slowly move across the surface. You think for a moment of the people down below who like you, will be going to bed now. You close your eyes and relax. As you relax you notice the slight whirring hum of the air conditioners? They make sure you and the others on the station have plenty of cool, fresh air. The humming sound helps you sleep, it's relaxing and nice to hear.

You will need to get a good night's sleep, as it will be a busy day tomorrow. You remember a supply ship from earth will be arriving and everyone on the space station will be busy unloading, sorting things out and putting them away. One thing about living on a space station is that everything has to be put away. You remember that anything left lying around will just float about, getting in the way. You close your eyes, you listen to the whirring sound. It is a gentle and relaxing sound. You think back over the day again, and for a moment you imagine the space station from the outside. It is clean and white, shining in the sunlight, with what look like big wings that are really to catch the sun and turn the light into electricity. It's beautiful above the blue and white Earth below. How special it is to be up here.

*** Okay (Childs name) it is time to rest now, and to relax? You know how, your good at relaxing. I think if you were really relaxed, anyone would think you were actually asleep. You may hear some of the sounds in the room, you can hear my voice but it doesn't bother you. You know how to relax, and enjoy the calm and quiet of bed time.

You can hear my voice, but that won't stop you relaxing, it's so easy to drift off into a restful sleep. You may feel as if your floating, letting go and really relaxing. Your arms and legs may start to feel heavy as you rest and relax.

Your eyes close, because your eyelids have started to feel heavy. Your whole body is starting to feel loose and heavy. It is a wonderful, warm feeling, to be so relaxed, to be comfortable and safe in your bed.

You feel so sleepy, you feel so comfortable and safe thinking about your day. (Childs name), you did so well today, only wonderful dreams will come. We all like to dream nice dreams and to feel safe and comfortable in our bed. You have started to feel that safe, comfortable, relaxed feeling now.

You know a restful night is coming, and you are pleased. That relaxed feeling is now spreading all around your body, from the bottom of your feet all the way up to the top of your head. You feel so very comfortable, relaxed and safe, both inside and outside. All the way through your body, it's a great feeling.

You may still hear the sounds in the room, my voice as I talk. But that doesn't bother you, you don't even notice it any more. You just rest, relax and enjoy that comfortable safe feeling in your bed. Tomorrow is another day, and you will wake up fresh and alert. But for now lets get a good, restful sleep.

***(Feel free to vary and repeat parts as you see fit. Try to use a gentle tone, and don't forget to use the child's name).

2 – A FLYING BOAT

A flying boat is an aircraft, but one that can take off and land on water. They look mostly like a plane, with wings and engines, but the bottom is like a boat. One of the great things about them is they can land anywhere there is calm water, such as a lake or in a bay. They don't need a runway like regular aircraft, though some also have wheels so they can land on a runway if they want too. Flying boats used to be very popular, but you don't see so many nowadays. They could be small, or very large. The one we are visiting is quite a large one. It has a cockpit up front, for two pilots. Behind the pilots is a small cabin for the radio operator and navigator. The navigator, who keeps an eye on where they are and where they need to be has a table for his maps. In the next section is what's called the engineer. He keeps an eye on the engines, and make adjustments if he needs to, even in flight. Then there is a small cabin just behind the engineer, and that has beds in it. The reason they have beds is that the flying boat can go on very long flights. Sometimes on long flights some of the crew needs a rest, even a sleep. Once in a while there may even be an extra pilot. He can take over when one of the others becomes tired. The tired pilot can then go into the sleeper cabin and have a sleep. Flying boats can be used on all sorts of jobs, from looking for any sailors who may have got lost to delivering supplies to small islands that may not have a runway. They can be very useful, and with their sweeping boat like shape, can be very beautiful.

It has been a busy day for you. Helping with a delivery run to a small island. With no airport or runway, the flying boat is the only way to land there. It was a long flight, and your now on the return journey, on your way home. It has been an hour since you took off, and its dark now. It is going to be quite a while before you get back, and as your job was helping unload and deliver the supplies, there is not much for you to do. One of the crew suggested you take a nap, maybe sleep for a while. That sounded a great idea, you did a lot of lifting of boxes, and some were heavy. You had to get them out of the flying boat, and onto the small wooden jetty the boat had stopped alongside. The local people were very nice and helped as much as they could. But as they were not allowed on the aircraft, in case they fell or tripped on things everything had to be lifted out to them. Your tired and love the chance to relax, maybe even get some restful sleep. You make your way back to the sleeper compartment. There is no door to open or close, more of a small hatchway to pass through. You have to duck down so as not to bump your head as you enter. Once inside you notice the light is on. Not a bright light, just a little round one overhead. You then notice the beds, there are three in all. One is on your right and on the other side are two bunk beds. You notice they have blankets and a pillow on each. There are also two small windows, one on each side. You climb into the one on your left. The bed seems to be a fold out type, so when not in use they can be folded up against the side of the aircraft. A good idea if you need some extra room, you though. You pull the covers over yourself and lean over to switch off the light. The switch was nearby, on the side of the bed. The compartment goes dark, but within a minute or two you realise the light from the next compartment is seeping in, so you can see quite well around the cabin. You look at the small window to your side, but only see darkness. Its night and with a little light in the cabin, you can't see anything. You think it will be great tomorrow to look out and see the sea passing underneath. For now though, it's time to get that much needed restful sleep. Time to lay back, shuffle about to get comfortable and close your eyes. You decide to listen. You hear the drone of the engines, it is a very relaxing sound. You can also just about hear a voice, it is one of the pilots asking the other if he wants a drink? You open your eyes and lean to one side, you can just about see the pilots up at the front, one is giving the other a cup of something. You lean back and close your eyes again, there is that wonderful relaxing humming of the engines. For a moment you imagine the sea plane from the outside, such a graceful and beautiful aircraft, flying high with the sea below, safely on its way.

*** Okay (Childs name) it is time to rest now, and to relax? You know how, your good at relaxing. I think if you were really relaxed, anyone would think you were actually asleep. You may hear some of the sounds in the room, you can hear my voice but it doesn't bother you. You know how to relax, to enjoy the calm and quiet of bed time.

You can hear my voice, but that won't stop you relaxing, it's so easy to drift off into a restful slsleep. You feel sleepy, you may feel as if your floating, letting go and really relaxing. Your arms and legs may start to feel heavy as you rest and relax.

Your eyes close, because your eyelids have started to feel heavy. Your whole body is starting to relax now, begining to feel loose and heavy. It is a wonderful, warm feeling, to be relaxed, to be comfortable and safe in your bed.

You feel so sleepy, you feel so comfortable and safe. (Childs name), you did so well today, only wonderful dreams will come. We all like to dream nice dreams and to feel safe and comfortable in our bed. You have started to feel that safe, comfortable, relaxed feeling now.

You know a restful night is coming, and you are pleased. That relaxed feeling is now spreading all around your body, from the bottom of your feet all the way up to the top of your head. You feel so very comfortable, relaxed and safe, both inside and outside. All the way through your body, it's a great feeling.

You may still hear the sounds in the room, my voice as I talk. But that doesn't bother you, you don't even notice it any more. You just rest, relax and enjoy that comfortable safe feeling in your bed. Tomorrow is another day, and you will wake up fresh and alert. But for now lets get a good, restful sleep.

***(Feel free to vary and repeat parts as you see fit. Try to use a gentle tone, and don't forget to use the child's name).

3 – IN A TENT

Camping with a tent can be fun, lots of people like camping. One thing about camping is you can be out in the countryside, by a lake or in a wood. Wherever you prefer. There are lots special camp sites in all sorts of places. When camping you can go almost anywhere and have a dry, comfortable and relaxing night's sleep. The next day you can explore the area, you can have fun discovering new places. It can be very relaxing and a bit of an adventure at the same time. Some people have small tents, just big enough for one or two people. Others have big tents, that actually have different rooms inside and can sleep a whole family. Whichever your using, you can be in the same camp site and it's going to be fun. It's going to be fun and relaxing.

The day started when you left home, and drove with the family to the camping site. It had been a long drive, and might have been a little boring but there were plenty of games to play in the car. One favourite was picking a colour of car. Then each person tried to spot other cars of that colour before anyone else saw them. The person who spotted five first, won. Sometimes the games were very quick, like when in traffic and surrounded by lots of cars. Other times, like on a big open country road surrounded by fields, it wasn't so quick, or easy. Sometimes you would get distracted and look away, then someone else beat you to it. Even when you were not playing games, it was great to watch the countryside pass by. Lots of green fields, woods and small villages to see.

By early evening you arrived at the camp site you would be spending the night at. It was bigger than you expected, and looked lovely. It was neat and tidy, a large open grassy area surrounded by trees. As you were unloading the tent from the car in you spotted a stream off behind some of the nearby trees. It would be fun to check that out later. The first thing however was to set up the tent. Once that was done you could really relax, knowing a safe and warm bed would be waiting for you at bed time.

Setting up the tent was great fun, and even though it fell down a couple of times, everyone laughed and enjoyed themselves. Once that had been done, it was time for a break and some sandwiches. Everyone sat in a circle by the tent and ate. As well as sandwiches there was some crunchy salad, some hard-boiled eggs and some drinks.

As soon as you could you had gone for a walk. You made straight for the stream you had noticed when you arrived. You had to pass through some trees before you could reach it. It looked lovely. The water gently trickling along was making a pleasant, relaxing sound. You sat on the bank and just watched and listened for some time. It was very relaxing, and you felt calm and happy to be there. You could have sat there for hours, but it started getting dark and you decided to return to the tent.

One of the best bits about camping is sleeping in a tent. Maybe it's the fresh air? Fresh air can be really relaxing, as can the sound of the breeze in the trees or pressing on the sides of the tent. It's very quiet at night in the countryside, there are none of the noises of the town. No sound of traffic, trains or people talking as they walk by. It was time for a good sleep. You went into the tent and changed for bed. You have your own small room inside the tent, all comfortable and dry and safe. There is a small window and a flap that hangs down to cover it. You have your own sleeping bag, thick and warm. You climb inside and wriggle about to get comfy. It feels great, comfortable and warm.

You lay back and think about the day you just had, it had been a great day. The journey had been fun, and the camp site looked lovely. You already visited the nearby stream, perhaps tomorrow you will take a longer walk. It was so green and air smelt so fresh here. It was so relaxing and the gentle sounds of the countryside helped. You think again about the day, it was great fun of putting the tent up. It took a few try's but it was worth it and how you laughed and enjoyed it.

You shuffle about a little, getting even more comfortable in the bed. You stop moving, trying to be as quiet as you can and you listen. What can you hear? There is a breeze finding any nook or cranny in the tent to whistle its way around, it is a gentle, relaxing sound. Maybe if you listen carefully you can also hear the water in the nearby stream you saw earlier. It's just a trickle, but made a pleasant and relaxing sound. You can also hear the occasional hoot of an owl. You decide that's a nice sound. It's getting colder outside with the night air but you are warm, cosy and safe inside.

And what about the next day? Lots to look forward to tomorrow. What will you do first? Maybe go back to the stream? You wonder if there are any fish in it? Perhaps if you sit by the side of the stream and stay rally still and quiet, you might see some? Time to sleep now though, just snuggle up warm and safe and listen to the breeze outside. You can't wait for tomorrow, but for now, you close your eyes and imagine the tent from the outside. The tent sides moving a little in the breeze, its dark but your safe and warm inside.

*** Okay (Childs name) it is time to rest now, and to relax? You know how, your good at relaxing. I think if you were really relaxed, anyone would think you were actually asleep. You may hear some of the sounds in the room, you can hear my voice but it doesn't bother you. You know how to relax, to enjoy the calm and quiet of bed time.

You can hear my voice, but that won't stop you relaxing, it's so easy to relax, to drift down into a restful sleep. You feel sleepy, you may even may feel as if your floating, letting go and really relaxing. Your arms and legs may start to feel heavy as you rest and relax.

Your eyes close, because your eyelids have started to feel heavy. Your whole body is starting to relax, to feel loose and heavy. It is a wonderful, warm feeling, to be relaxed, to be comfortable and safe in your bed.

You feel so sleepy, you feel so comfortable and safe. (Childs name), you did so well today, only wonderful dreams will come. We all like to dream nice dreams and to feel safe and comfortable in our bed. You have started to feel that safe, comfortable, relaxed feeling now.

You know a restful night is coming, and you are pleased. That relaxed feeling is now spreading all around your body, from the bottom of your feet all the way up to the top of your head. You feel so very comfortable and safe, both inside and outside. All the way through your body, it's a great feeling.

You may still hear the sounds in the room, my voice as I talk. But that doesn't bother you, you don't even notice it any more. You just rest, relax and enjoy that comfortable safe feeling in your bed. Tomorrow is another day, and you will wake up fresh and alert. But for now lets get a good, restful sleep.

***(Feel free to vary and repeat parts as you see fit. Try to use a gentle tone, and don't forget to use the child's name).

◆ ◆ ◆

4 – OLD SAILING SHIP

Old sailing ships were made of wood, and have been built for hundreds of years. They have no engines, but use the wind in huge canvas sails to move along. The sailors of those old ships were very skilled and would often make long journeys. The old sailing ships in fact managed to sail completely around the world, using just the wind and sails to power them along.

They sailed much more slowly than ships of today do, with their modern engines. A skilled sailor could use even a little wind, sometimes even a wind going in a different direction to the one they wanted. To do that they took a sort of zig zag route. Of course, if the wind stopped completely, the ship would also stop. Then they would have to wait for the wind to pick up again, though out on the wide flat ocean that didn't happen too often. Even having to use the wind, the old wooden ships still managed to sail far and wide, discovering new lands and animals as they went. Countries like Australia and America were found by men in wooden sailing ships, along with new and interesting animals. Sometimes they even met people that the sailors had never seen before. It was a time of discovery as they learned much more about our world, and the wooden sailing ships were the way they travelled.

The ship we are visiting is one of the old wooden sailing ships. It had been wonderful to see when you first arrived. Tied to the harbour wall, the ship was bigger and taller than you expected. The large cloth sails were tied up, gathered against the cross spars, which is what they call the wood beams the sails hang from. Once unfurled, they would fill with the wind and carry the ship along. You counted three tall masts, and you also saw what seemed miles of ropes going in all directions. The ropes are called the rigging, and attached to the tall, towering masts and cross spars. Men can pull on some of the ropes to control the sails from the deck below. That was hard work, but they managed very well.

You had spent the day exploring the ship. First, walking around on the wooden deck, which was great fun. You imagines being the captain, sailing far out at sea. Next, you went below, as they call the lower decks. At first, coming from the bright daylight above it seemed dark and you could hardly see anything. After a minute or two however while your eyes got used to it, you could see clearly. The ceilings were low, much lower than a normal room in a house. You noticed a little wind, and saw the windows were open. The windows were quite small and square, with wooden shutters, like little doors to close across them. The wind was welcome, as the below the deck the ship felt a little stuffy and warm.

The sides of the ship looked curved, not at all like the walls of your room at home, all flat and straight. The first floor, or deck as they call it was originally for the cannons. There are none there now, though the little square windows thay would look out from were still there. The next deck down is where you will sleep, and as it turns out, having spent a lot of time exploring it's time for bed, and a real surprise.

The bed is a traditional sailor's bed, it is hanging from the roof with ropes and called a hammock. You got into it by pulling yourself up and lowering yourself into it. Nothing like climbing into your bed at home. It seemed really very odd at first, but once inside you had the next surprise, it was so comfortable relaxing you almost fell asleep right away. The hammock sort of wrapped itself around you, making you feel very snug, cosy and safe. You shift about a little, getting really comfortable and notice the hammock starts to swing, just a little. That felt really nice, and you already knew you're going to get a great night's sleep. Then you try to stay very still and listen to the sounds around you. The sea is calm and the ship is very gently swaying from side to side. It's a relaxing feeling and you think it's a bit like being rocked to sleep. The first sound you notice is a gentle creaking sound, a little like an old door or garden gate might when opening and closing. The sound is the wood the ship is made of moving a little as the ship rocks gently from side to side. It's a relaxing sound, a sort of gentle sound. As you close your eyes you imagine the ship itself, from the outside. It is rolling gently as the swell of the sea pass's underneath. You notice the occasional slap of the water as it breaks gently against the side of the ship.

It's time to think about your day, exploring the old wooden ship. Up and down the stairs you climbed, exploring one deck after another. Each a little different, but each with low ceilings and huge wooden beams everywhere. It was so exciting and interesting. Next, you think about tomorrow. Tomorrow the ship will go for a short sail, around to the next port. It will be great to see the huge sails filled out with the wind and to watch the sea, with its white topped waves dancing up and down. The sails and the ropes will all come together to make a wonderful flapping sound as the wind fills them. You can hardly wait. Tomorrow will be a great day. For now though, it's a good night's sleep that's needed. Time to relax and think of the ship, the day you just had and the one you're looking forward to tomorrow.

** Okay (Childs name) it is time to rest now, and to relax? You know how, your good at relaxing. I think if you were really relaxed, anyone would think you were actually asleep. You may hear some of the sounds in the room, you can hear my voice but it doesn't bother you. You know how to relax, to enjoy the calm and quiet of bed time.

You can hear my voice, but that won't stop you relaxing, it's so easy to relax, to drift down into a restful sleep. You feel sleepy, you may even feel as if your floating, letting go and really relaxing. Your arms and legs may start to feel heavy as you rest and relax.

Your eyes close, because your eyelids have started to feel heavy. Your whole body is starting to relax, to feel loose and heavy. It is a wonderful, warm feeling, to be relaxed, to be comfortable and safe in your bed.

You feel so sleepy, you feel so comfortable and safe. (Childs name), you did so well today, only wonderful dreams will come. We all like to dream nice dreams and feel safe and comfortable in our bed. You have started to feel that safe, comfortable, relaxed feeling now.

You know a restful night is coming, and you are pleased. That relaxed feeling is now spreading all around your body, from the bottom of your feet all the way up to the top of your head. You feel so very comfortable, relaxed and safe, both inside and outside. All the way through your body, it's a great feeling.

You may still hear the sounds in the room, my voice as I talk. But that doesn't bother you, you don't even notice it any more. You just rest, relax and enjoy that comfortable safe feeling in your bed. Tomorrow is another day, and you will wake up fresh and alert. But for now lets get a good, restful sleep.

***(Feel free to vary and repeat parts as you see fit. Try to use a gentle tone, and don't forget to use the child's name).

◆ ◆ ◆

5 – IN A CASTLE (4 POSTER BED)

Castles are very big and strong buildings, they were built hundreds of years ago to keep the people inside safe. They were usually built of huge stone blocks, though the first ones were built of wood. Some castles are tall and very large with room for many hundreds of people inside. Most of them have a tall outer wall, going right around with towers in each corner. In the middle there would be an open area, called a courtyard and often another large stone building in the middle, called the keep.

The keep would have been the heart of the castle, and in there would have been lots of rooms and one great big one, often called the great hall. That's where everyone would have meals and talk together. Some castles even had a water filled ditch around the castle to make them even safer. That was called a moat. Not all of them had a moat, but the one you are visiting does. There is a bridge over it into the castle. In olden times the bridge could have been removed, to prevent anyone who wasn't welcome from coming in. Once over the bridge you will have to pass through the gate, and the gate is set into a sort of mini castle, to defend the gate and protect everyone inside. Of course, that was hundreds of years ago, and now the only people to pass through the gate are visitors, having a good, relaxing and restful day out exploring.

Tonight, you will be sleeping in the castle which is going to be a real treat. You spent the whole day looking around. The entrance gate was huge and very impressive, to get to it you walked over the wooden bridge. You remember looking down and seeing the water of the moat, passing around the castle. It looked very nice, the water was twinkling in the sunshine and you watched some ducks swimming by. Once over the bridge you walked towards the gate. There were huge wooden doors that could be closed, but they were open for you and the other visitors. It went a little dark as you walked through the gateway. It was a sort of short tunnel with stone walls and felt cool inside.

The first thing you noticed as you passed through the gate was a large building in the middle of the castle. The Keep. It looked very tall and strong, almost like a mini castle inside the bigger castle. You looked around the sides of the outer wall next, at the top of the wall was a walkway, a path so anyone could see outside easily. In the corners were towers, tall stone towers. You counted them, and could see four, one in each corner. You looked up and saw some people had climbed the stairs to the top of one, and were taking pictures. That seemed a great idea, and into the tower you went. The stairs were very odd. They were in a spiral, so you sort of walked around in circles while going up. It was great that someone had thought of running a thick rope around the edge of the wall, for holding on too. It had been a little awkward when you met some other people coming down. You had to squeeze a little to one side as they passed. It was very narrow. It had been hard work, there were a lot of stairs but like the entrance gate, it was cool and shaded in the stairway so had not been too difficult.

Once at the top you could see right away it had been worth the climb. The view was great and looking inward you could see the whole castle from there. The big keep in the middle and the walls around it. You could even see the other towers, and the main gate. Looking down you noticed other visitors walking around in the courtyard. You were quite high and they look small from up there. If you turned and looked out, away from the castle. You could see for miles. Rolling hills and some woods, off into the distance. It looked amazing, and you thought about how special it would be to spend the night there. A very special treat indeed.

After a very nice tea, you were shown the room you would sleep in. The first surprise on entering the bedroom was the bed, it is a four poster bed. What's a four poster bed? It's a bed with four posts of course, one in each corner and a sort of roof on top. In the old days in cold, stone castles they would close curtains around the bed, to help keep it warm and stop any drafts.

You climb into the bed. Its softer than you expect, and very comfortable. You pull the cover up over you and take a look around. Its dark, but you can still see quite well. We don't need the curtains around the bed closed tonight, the covers are warm and the bed very comfy. You can see the stone walls of the room, not like the walls at home at all. Big and grey, they look very strong and will certainly keep any bad weather out. It's very quiet, and no noise at all can be heard. Its very relaxing and closing your eyes you might imagine the castle form the outside, tall and strong, the stone walls keeping everyone inside safe and comfortable.

You decide it is now time to sleep.

*** Okay (Childs name) it is time to rest now, and to relax? You know how, your good at relaxing. I think if you were really relaxed, anyone would think you were actually asleep. You may hear some of the sounds in the room, you can hear my voice but it doesn't bother you. You know how to relax, to enjoy the calm and quiet of bed time.

You can hear my voice, but that won't stop you relaxing, it's so easy to relax, to drift down into a restful sleep. You may feel as if your floating, letting go and really relaxing. Your arms and legs may start to feel heavy as you rest and relax.

Your eyes close, because your eyelids have started to feel heavy. Your whole body is starting to relax now, to feel loose and heavy. It is a wonderful, warm feeling, to be relaxed, to be comfortable and safe in your bed.

You feel so sleepy, you feel so comfortable and safe. (Childs name), you did so well today, only wonderful dreams will come. We all like to dream nice dreams and to feel safe and comfortable in our bed. You have started feeling that safe, comfortable, relaxed feeling now.

You know a restful night is coming, and you are pleased. That relaxed feeling is now spreading all around your body, from the bottom of your feet all the way up to the top of your head. You feel so very comfortable, relaxed and safe, both inside and outside. All the way through your body, it's a great feeling.

You may still hear the sounds in the room, my voice as I talk. But that doesn't bother you, you don't even notice it any more.

You just rest, relax and enjoy that comfortable safe feeling in your bed. Tomorrow is another day, and you will wake up fresh and alert. But for now lets get a good, restful sleep.

***(Feel free to vary and repeat parts as you see fit. Try to use a gentle tone, and don't forget to use the child's name).

6 – ON A TRAIN

Trains are made up of a series of wheeled carriages that run on steel tracks. They run regularly in almost every country in the world and carry passengers as well as freight. People take trains to and from work, but also on holiday, visiting friends and for many other reasons. The power for the train comes from the engine at the front. Older trains were powered by hot steam and would leave white clouds as they travelled along. The carriages they pull carrying people are also called coaches. Like the old horse drawn coaches that used to carry passengers on the roads.

Some train journeys are quick, perhaps travelling only a short distance. Other journeys can go on for hours, and some really long-distance trips can last several days. On many of the long-distance trips, the train might have a restaurant car, or café. People can order food and drink, even sitting down at a table for a lovely meal.

On many of those longer journeys, the passengers will also sleep. Sometimes they will sleep in their seats, sometimes they will lay down, longways on the bench seat if there is the room. Maybe using their bag or rolled coat as a pillow. Sometimes though on special long-distance train journeys there are proper sleeper cabins. Often called compartments. These are small rooms that contain a bed, often with a little bathroom. The beds can be fixed, others might fold down from the wall giving the passenger more room during the day. The beds can be very comfortable, and the sounds of the train moving over the rails along with the slow, gentile sway of the carriage is very relaxing. Clickety clack, clickety clack. The sound of a train on the move. That sound is from the wheels as they pass over the joins in the rails.

Tonight, you are in a special sleeper compartment on a train. The compartment is small, much smaller than your room at home but clean, neat and well laid out. You look around the compartment, there is a bed which looks very comfortable. You see a small table next to the bed and a little shelf alongside it. Above table is a small mirror, with a light above it and a cord hanging down to switch it on. On the opposite side of the compartment to the bed is a narrow sliding door, and inside that is a real surprise, a small bathroom. Now you didn't expect that. You notice the sound, a clickety clack of the train wheels. The sound is very relaxing. Next, you change for bed and brush your teeth.

You feel tired, very tired. It's time to climb into the bed and get comfortable. Once in the bed you pull the cover up, how comfortable and relaxing it feels. You move about a little, to get as comfortable as possible. As you do so, you relax and start to think about the day you just had. You remember having lunch and tea on the train, in the very smart restaurant carriage. The food had been lovely. You remember sitting in the comfortable seat, watching to world pass by. The fields, trees and sometimes farms. It had been very nice to watch, and very relaxing. Next you think about tomorrow and arriving at the station in the morning. It will be good to get there but for now, it feels great to be warm, safe and comfortable in the bed.

You glance about the little compartment. You see the little table. On it is your tooth brush and tooth paste. You reach over to the light switch, and turn the compartment light off. As you lay back into the bed, once again you notice the clickety clack of the train as it runs along. You can feel a slight movement as the carriage rocks from side to side, but only a little. For a few moments you imagine the train from the outside, running along through the night, the engine pulling the train, the wheels going around. The clickety clack of the wheels is a nice sound, it is really very relaxing so you lay back and relax, it is time to sleep.

** Okay (Childs name) it is time to rest now, and to relax? You know how, your good at relaxing. I think if you were really relaxed, anyone would think you were actually asleep. You may hear some of the sounds in the room, you can hear my voice but it doesn't bother you. You know how to relax, to enjoy the calm and quiet of bed time.

You can hear my voice, but that won't stop you relaxing, it's so easy to relax, to drift down into a restful sleep. You may may even feel as if your floating, letting go and really relaxing. Your arms and legs may start to feel heavy as you rest and relax.

Your eyes close, because your eyelids have started to feel heavy. Your whole body is starting to relax, to feel loose and heavy. It is a wonderful, warm feeling, to be relaxed, to be comfortable and safe in your bed.

You feel so sleepy, you feel so comfortable and safe. (Childs name), you did so well today, only wonderful dreams will come. We all like to dream nice dreams and to feel safe, comfortable in our bed. You have started to feel that safe, comfortable, relaxed feeling now.

You know a restful night is coming, and you are pleased. That relaxed feeling is now spreading all around your body, from the bottom of your feet all the way up to the top of your head. You feel so very comfortable and safe, both inside and outside. All the way through your body, it's a great feeling.

You may still hear the sounds in the room, my voice as I talk. But that doesn't bother you, you don't even notice it any more. You just rest, relax and enjoy that comfortable safe feeling in your bed. Tomorrow is another day, and you will wake up fresh and alert. But for now lets get a good, restful sleep.

***(Feel free to vary and repeat parts as you see fit. Try to use a gentle tone, and don't forget to use the child's name).

◆ ◆ ◆

7 – IN A CAMPER VAN

Camper vans are great, they are bigger than a car, and about the size of a small van. Unlike a van though most have windows and beds inside. There are many different types, some are small while others can be very large. The smaller ones might just have a bed in the back, while the larger ones can have two or more beds. On some the beds can also be used as benches for sitting on during the day. Camper vans sometimes have a small kitchen, a fridge, a little bathroom and even a TV. Some of the smaller ones even have a roof that expands upwards when they are parked, to give the people inside more space to stand. You can even have a sort of tent that folds out from the side, giving the campers somewhere to sit, to protect them from the bright sunshine on a hot day.

Sometimes you can see the camper vans driving along on the road. Many will have a special holder on the back for bicycles.

The idea is that once parked in the camp site, the owners can go off on the bikes and explore the local area, pop to a nearby beach or shady wood. Anywhere they want really. Another great thing about camper vans is that you get to take your own things from home. Your own bedding, your favourite cup and pretty much anything you want to take along. For many the camper van becomes like another room in their own house, just one that can drive away and visit somewhere interesting and fun.

Today you travelled many miles, and saw lots of wonderful things. You passed lots of open country, hills and woods, going over bridges and through valleys. Once in a while you drove through small towns, all windy roads and past old, stone houses. Some of the houses were thatched. That's a roof made of straw. They can be very pretty. The old houses and farms were nice to see, but you really liked the open countryside the best. You could see for miles and as you travelled along the views would change. Always something new to see.

It was a long day and a little tiring, but eventually you arrived at the camp site. It was a camp site specially for camper vans, and as you went in you could see a few others parked about. One was smaller than yours, some the same size and a couple that were much bigger. You saw one family sitting outside theirs, they were having their tea and all looked very happy and relaxed. Once parked and settled you had your tea. It was lovely and you enjoyed it, being quite hungry. After you had finished you decided to take a short walk around the camp site, just to stretch your legs and enjoy the cool fresh evening air. That was very restful and the fresh air seemed to clear your mind and relax you as you walked.

Your back at the camper van now, and have changed and brushed your teeth. You climbed into bed and pulled the covers up around yourself. You shuffle about a little to get really comfortable. It's getting colder outside with the night air but in the bed, you are toasty warm. Warm and comfortable, and very relaxed. You look along inside the camper van. You can see the front seats and also the top of the steering wheel. You look up to one side. There is a window, but it has a little curtain that you pulled closed earlier. It is dark in the van, it's very restful and relaxing. You feel safe and comfortable.

As you lay back and relax you think about the day, all the interesting things you saw on the way here. Next, you think about tomorrow and all the things you will get to see and do. Someone said there was a beautiful a waterfall nearby, and you know you will love to see that. Would it be a small, pretty waterfall, or a huge great thing going up a long way? You tried to picture it in your mind. Next you picture the camper van from the outside, parked close to the trees in the dark, with you all safe, warm and comfortable inside. Now though, it is time to lay back and close your eyes. It is time to get comfortable and relax. Time for a good, restful night's sleep.

** Okay (Childs name) it is time to rest now, and to relax? You know how, your good at relaxing. I think if you were really relaxed, anyone would think you were actually asleep. You may hear some of the sounds in the room, you can hear my voice but it doesn't bother you. You know how to relax, to enjoy the calm and quiet of bed time.

You can hear my voice, but that won't stop you relaxing, it's so easy to relax, to drift down into a restful sleep. You feel sleepy, you may even feel as if your floating, letting go and really relaxing. Your arms and legs may start to feel heavy as you rest and relax.

Your eyes close, because your eyelids have started to feel heavy.

Your whole body is starting to relax, to feel loose and heavy. It is a wonderful, warm feeling, to be relaxed, to be comfortable and safe in your bed.

You feel so sleepy, you feel so comfortable and safe. (Childs name), you did so well today, only wonderful dreams will come. We all like to dream nice dreams and to feel safe and comfortable in our bed. You have started to feel that safe, comfortable, relaxed feeling now.

You know a restful night is coming, and you are pleased. That relaxed feeling is now spreading all around your body, from the bottom of your feet all the way up to the top of your head. You feel so very comfortable, relaxed and safe, both inside and outside. All the way through your body, it's a great feeling.

You may still hear the sounds in the room, my voice as I talk. But that doesn't bother you, you don't even notice it any more. You just rest, relax and enjoy that comfortable safe feeling in your bed. Tomorrow is another day, and you will wake up fresh and alert. But for now, lets get a good, restful sleep.

***(Feel free to vary and repeat parts as you see fit. Try to use a gentle tone, and don't forget to use the child's name).

❖ ❖ ❖

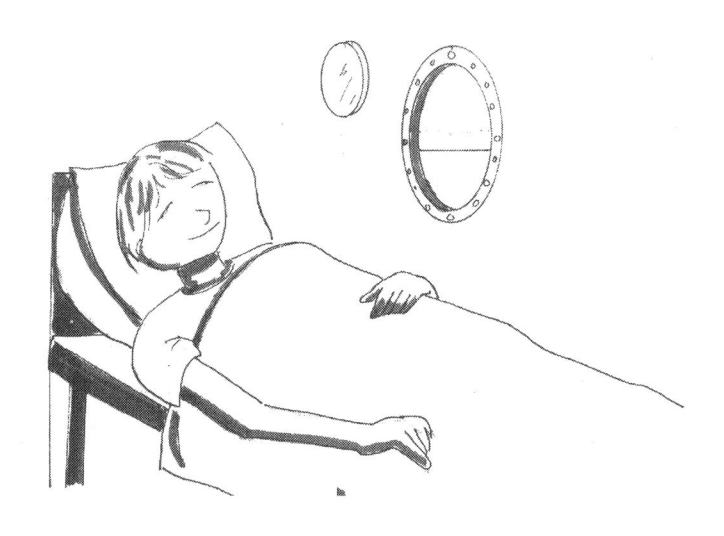

8 – ON A CRUSE SHIP

Cruise ships are large ships designed to take passengers on sailing holidays. They mostly sail on planned routes, so that the passengers can visit interesting places every time they stop. Cruise ships can be big or small, the largest can carry thousands of people and have lots of comfortable cabins for the guests. They can also have shops, restaurants, swimming pools. Some of the bigger cruise ships even have cinemas, theatres with shows and even kids' clubs. The Cruise ships are very much like a huge hotel, but at sea.

One of the great things about a cruise is all the different things you can see, both while at sea, and also when visiting interesting places. Another great thing is how comfortable and safe the ships are. Many even have a little hospital with a doctor and nurses, in case you feel unwell. The cabins are clean and neat, with beds, bathrooms and in some cases, a window to watch the sea pass by as you sail along. They really are relaxing and restful, and the crew are always around to help make your cruise as safe and comfortable as possible.

On your cruise you have spent the day exploring a lovely old town. The old stone buildings and scenery with the mountains in the distance were very enjoyable to see. You had a lovely lunch and have now returned to the ship. Once on board you joined your friends for dinner. A wonderful meal in one of the many relaxing restaurants to choose from.

After eating, you took a walk around the deck. The evening air was fresh, restful and relaxing. Then you returned to your cabin for the night. The cabin is about the same size as your bedroom at home. There is a comfortable bed, a small bathroom to one side and a table with two chairs. There is a round window that looks out over the sea. And as you get ready for bed, you notice the ship has started to sail again. The ship is rolling just a little, and you take a look out of the window. Its dark now, but there is enough light to see the sea shimmering in the moonlight as the light of the moonlight catches the wave tops.

You realise you are very tired. The evening meal was wonderful, and you enjoyed the restful walk. It had been very relaxing. You decide it is time for bed, and you climb in pulling the covers over yourself. They are clean and comfortable, and you can't help but relax as you think back over the day. Your mind goes to what you will do tomorrow. You the ship will be at sea, and you will have so much to choose from, so much you can do. Maybe a visit to the swimming pool? Or possibly go and see a film? The have cinemas on board. You so enjoyed the walk earlier in the evening, you decide to spend the day, or perhaps some of it just walking around the wide, long decks. Watching the sea pass by, and perhaps spotting any other ships that might be passing. That sounds like a great idea.

You look about the cabin, it is dark, but there is enough light to pick out the table and chair, and the window. The curtain is closed but around the edge you can see the shimmering glow of the moonlight. You lay back in the bed, shuffle about a little to get nice and comfortable and close your eyes. For a moment you imagine the ship from the outside. The huge ship gliding smoothly through the waves. The spray at the front as the ship breaks through the swell of the sea. You imagine all the passengers, going to sleep in their cabins. How relaxing it feels. Then you think about the crew, still looking after the ship, even at night. How safe it makes you feel. You can feel the slight vibration of the engines, it's a relaxing feeling. You feel safe, warm and comfortable, relaxing in your bed.

*** Okay (Childs name) it is time to rest now, and to relax? You know how, your good at relaxing. I think if you were really relaxed, anyone would think you were actually asleep. You may hear some of the sounds in the room, you can hear my voice but it doesn't bother you. You know how to relax, to enjoy the calm and quiet of bed time.

You can hear my voice, but that won't stop you relaxing, it's so easy to relax, to drift down into a restful sleep. You feel sleepy, you may even feel as if your floating, letting go and really relaxing. Your arms and legs may start to feel heavy as you rest and relax.

Your eyes close, because your eyelids have started to feel heavy. Your whole body is starting to relax, to feel loose and heavy. It is a wonderful, warm feeling, to be relaxed, to be comfortable and safe in your bed.

You feel so sleepy, you feel so comfortable and safe. (Childs name), you did so well today, only wonderful dreams will come. We all like to dream nice dreams and to feel safe, comfortable, and relaxed. You have started to feel that safe, comfortable, relaxed feeling now.

You know a restful night is coming, and you are pleased. That relaxed feeling is now spreading all around your body, from the bottom of your feet all the way up to the top of your head. You feel so very comfortable, relaxed and safe, both inside and outside. All the way through your body, it's a great feeling.

You may still hear the sounds in the room, my voice as I talk. But that doesn't bother you, you don't even notice it any more. You just rest, relax and enjoy that comfortable safe feeling in your bed. Tomorrow is another day, and you will wake up fresh and alert. But for now lets get a good, restful sleep.

***(Feel free to vary and repeat parts as you see fit. Try to use a gentle tone, and don't forget to use the child's name).

◆ ◆ ◆

9 – IN A LOG CABIN

A log cabin is a small building made of wooden logs. Lots of logs are fitted to together to make the walls and roof. They are often found out in the countryside, where the trees for wood is easily found. You won't find many log cabins in a town or city. They can be very strong and safe, and many are used as a holiday house, somewhere to spend a few days when out in the country or forests. They can also be used by rangers, the people who look after woods and forests. There are lots of different types, some large and some quite small.

Inside they can be very comfortable and warm, some having a stone or brick fireplace with a chimney that runs up the outside of the cabin. Some have several rooms, like a house, while others have just one big space. Tonight, you will be sleeping in a log cabin.

Today you were walking through the woods with friends. It has been a long walk, and you a carried some of your things in your back pack. You had stopped for a break at lunch time and eaten the sandwiches and snacks you had brought along. You were really glad to take a break, walking for a long time can be hard. You tired and needed a break. It was lovely sitting under the trees. It was a warm day, but cool and shady under the trees. Very restful and relaxing.

Walking through the woods can be fun, and the person with you knew the way well. You both stuck to the path, so there was no chance of going the wrong way. The woods can be confusing, not being too sure which way is which. But a good guide keeps everyone safe. It was great fun walking through the woods. The trees were wonderful, some small and others really huge. Reaching up towards the sky the sunlight played on the treetops, sometimes flickering on the ground as the wind moved the branches. There were lots of different sounds, all of which were very relaxing. The sound of the breeze weaving through the branches and leaves, the sounds of animals, mostly birds sitting in the trees or flying around above calling one another. At one point you saw some squirrels running around hight up in the branches. It was really surprising how they could run on such thin branches. You thought they would surely break and the squirrel fall, but that never happened.

It had been the early evening when you arrived at the log cabin. It appeared slowly as you came out of the trees. It was set in a small clearing and looked wonderful. The cabin was a lovely deep brown colour, the walls were made of wood logs, set one on top of the other. The roof was made of wood as well. You could see the front door and several windows. Then you noticed a brick chimney at the other end of the cabin. It all looked lovey, sitting in the clearing and with the sunlight bouncing off the roof it almost seemed to have a warm glow. It looked very strong and safe. You really looked forward to a good night's sleep in the log cabin.

Soon after getting inside you realised it was time to go to bed. You were happy about that, being tired after the long day. After getting changed and brushing your teeth you climbed into bed. It was a wooden bed with colourful, patterned covers and a big, soft pillow. Once in the bed you pulled the covers up around yourself. You shuffled about a little, to get really comfortable, and looked about the room. It was dark, but there was enough light to pick out the wood walls, and the window with a curtain that was now closed. You shut your eyes and listened. It was very quiet, but you could hear a hooting noise, from off in the forest. It was a sort of whoop sound and had to be the owls. Of course, out in the woods there would be owl's, and they come out at night after sleeping through the day. It was a pleasant sound, a relaxing sound. Next you imagined the log cabin from the outside, sitting in the clearing, surrounded by trees picked out by the moonlight. You thought for a moment about tomorrow, so much to look forward too, more exploring in the woods for a start. For now though, it was time for a good nights sleep.

*** Okay (Childs name) it is time to rest now, and to relax? You know how, your good at relaxing. I think if you were really relaxed, anyone would think you were actually asleep. You may hear some of the sounds in the room, you can hear my voice but it doesn't bother you. You know how to relax, to enjoy the calm and quiet of bed time.

You can hear my voice, but that won't stop you relaxing, it's so easy to relax, to drift down into a restful sleep. You feel sleepy, you may even feel as if your floating, letting go and really relaxing. Your arms and legs may start to feel heavy as you rest and relax.

Your eyes close, because your eyelids have started to feel heavy. Your whole body is starting to relax, to feel loose and heavy. It is a wonderful, warm feeling, to be relaxed, to be comfortable and safe in your bed.

You feel so sleepy, you feel so comfortable and safe. (Childs name), you did so well today, only wonderful dreams will come. We all like to dream nice dreams and to feel safe, comfortable in our bed. You have started to feel that safe, comfortable, relaxed feeling now.

You know a restful night is coming, and you are pleased. That relaxed feeling is now spreading all around your body, from the bottom of your feet all the way up to the top of your head. You feel so very comfortable, relaxed and safe, both inside and outside. All the way through your body, it's a great feeling.

You may still hear the sounds in the room, my voice as I talk. But that doesn't bother you, you don't even notice it any more. You just rest, relax and enjoy that comfortable safe feeling in your bed. Tomorrow is another day, and you will wake up fresh and alert. But for now lets get a good, restful sleep.

***(Feel free to vary and repeat parts as you see fit. Try to use a gentle tone, and don't forget to use the child's name).

◆ ◆ ◆

10 - MOON BASE

A moon base is an outpost on the moon. Sometimes called a Lunar Outpost, it is a series of buildings, called modules, all connected together. It has to be airtight, as there is no air on the moon. The inside is very comfortable, air conditioned and warm. There is a big crew on the moon base, they live and work there, usually for a year at a time. Then, after a year they come back to Earth and someone else goes there. The moon base is very comfortable, apart from the work modules there are sleeping modules and a restaurant. The food is great, with all sorts of tasty things to choose from. The sleeping modules are very comfortable and relaxing. Each person has their own small cabin, a little like being on a ship. In each cabin is a comfortable bed and small bathroom room. Some of the workers go outside, in space suits and wheeled vehicles, so they can get quite dirty. With them returning after hours outside and the important scientific experiments some do, keeping everything and everyone clean is really important.

The crew here do lots of different things. There are scientists who study the moon, and outer space with telescopes. There are engineers who study life in space, and do experiments on how to make the base better, and study how we might travel to other planets, like Mars.

The whole place is clean and tidy, it has to be as any mess can cause lots of problems. The bedrooms, or cabins are also clean and tidy, but there can be some personal items. One person you know has a small bear that reminds them of home. Another had a snow globe, they can shake it and reminds them of snow, like they get back home on Earth. One person likes to play the sound of rain as well as music, although it can't rain on the moon it reminds them of home.

The cabins are not big, but there is enough room for a bed and side table, along with a cupboard for clothes and shoes. The bed even has draws underneath. You need all the space you can for extra clothes. Along one wall is a shelf. One side has some books, while the other has some personal bits, a note book, some pens and a small torch, in case you want to find something in the dark. To the side of the room, behind a sliding door is a small bathroom. In there you keep your soap, shampoo and of course, your tooth paste and tooth brush.

It has been a long and busy day and your tired. You change and brush your teeth. You climb into bed. It feels so good to snuggle under the cover and relax at last. You remember it will be another busy day tomorrow, lots of things to organise as a supply ship will be arriving from earth. There will be supplies, like food and equipment to unload, and then the ship will be taking a couple of people back with it to earth. It is not your turn to go yet though.

You're up here for a few weeks yet. Your pleased about that, this is really different and you enjoy being here.

The only thing to do right now though is to relax, shut your eyes and think about the moon base, and maybe your friends back on earth. Laying back relaxing you take a look around the cabin. It is dark but there is enough light to pick out the shelf, with some of your favourite books. You can see the small table and next to it, the cupboard. Next you notice the door to the bathroom. It is closed.

You shut your eyes, and for a moment imagine the moon base from the outside. The moon is grey and dusty, then sitting there amoung the rocks all bright and white is the moon base. A series of different modules, all joined together. You imagine how it looks with the lights on, there are windows so the lights can easily be seen. Some are spreading pools of light onto the ground outside. You can see some little flashing lights, red ones dotted about the moon base. Those are so anyone can see where it is, even from a distance. You close your eyes, it's time to sleep.

*** Okay (Childs name) it is time to rest now, and to relax? You know how, your good at relaxing. I think if you were really relaxed, anyone would think you were actually asleep. You may hear some of the sounds in the room, you can hear my voice but it doesn't bother you. You know how to relax, to enjoy the calm and quiet of bed time.

You can hear my voice, but that won't stop you relaxing, it's so easy to relax, to drift down into a restful sleep. You feel sleepy, you may even feel as if your floating, letting go and really relaxing. Your arms and legs may start to feel heavy as you rest and relax.

Your eyes close, because your eyelids have started to feel heavy. Your whole body is starting to relax, to feel loose and heavy. It is a wonderful, warm feeling, to be relaxed, to be comfortable and safe in your bed.

You feel so sleepy, you feel so comfortable and safe. (Childs name), you did so well today, only wonderful dreams will come. We all like to dream nice dreams and to feel safe, comfortable in our bed.

You have started to feel that safe, comfortable, relaxed feeling now.

You know a restful night is coming, and you are pleased. That relaxed feeling is now spreading all around your body, from the bottom of your feet all the way up to the top of your head. You feel so very comfortable and safe, both inside and outside. All the way through your body, it's a great feeling.

You may still hear the sounds in the room, my voice as I talk. But that doesn't bother you, you don't even notice it any more. You just rest, relax and enjoy that comfortable safe feeling in your bed. Tomorrow is another day, and you will wake up fresh and alert. But for now lets get a good, restful sleep.

***(Feel free to vary and repeat parts as you see fit. Try to use a gentle tone, and don't forget to use the child's name).

◆ ◆ ◆

11 – A PASSENGER AIRLINER

Aircraft fly all over the world, often from one country to another. They carry all sorts of things, people of course but also cargo, sometimes called freight. Freight are goods that can include almost anything from medical supplies to food and pretty much anything you can imagine. When carrying people there are seats, quite comfortable ones and arranged in rows with a space, or aisle down the middle. They have wash rooms and on longer flights serve food to the passengers. On very long flights several meals might be served, breakfast, lunch and even dinner. Some of the smaller airliners will carry about 100 passengers, but the larger ones can carry many more. There have been passenger planes around for a long time, the first flying over 100 years ago.

People fly for work, they fly for holidays and many do so because they are the aircraft crews. Flight times vary a lot, some journeys can be short, others very long and it's on those that people often need to sleep. What most of the passengers don't realise while sleeping in their seats is that the crew have their own private little sleeping cabins at the top of the plane. There is a secret staircase and above the passenger compartments are several smaller compartments with beds. These are called Crew Rest Compartments. The crew on long journeys will often take turns working, looking after the passengers, serving food or flying the plane. Those not working can go up into the little cabin and have a restful, relaxing sleep.

It has been a long day and you are on the airliner because you're a special guest, you have also been allowed to use the crew rest compartment as a special treat. You had to pass through a small doorway and climb a narrow, turning staircase. At the top you found a small open space, around which were several small sleeping compartments. They were set side by side, and each had a bed inside with curtains that could be closed. You looked more closely and could see a very comfortable looking bed. There are blankets and pillows, the bed looked clean and very neat. You noticed a switch and pressed it, a small light above your head came on, then you pressed it again and it turned off. That will be handy when the curtain is closed, you thought.

Just then another member of the crew arrived. The crew member said they were going to have a sleep, and climbed into one of the compartments at the far end. He said he hoped you had a good sleep, and pulled the curtain closed. You did the same, climbing inside and closing the curtain. It seemed quite dark, then you remembered the little light, which you turned on. You are very tired and really needed a good sleep, so you slip under the covers, and shift about a little getting really comfortable.

You lay back and relax at last. You look about, you see the small compartment, it looks very comfortable and safe. You notice the curtain, it is swaying slightly with the movement of the aircraft. You decide to switch off the light, and having done that you shift about a little more. You are really comfortable now, and starting to relax even more. You start to listen. You can hear the noise of the airliners engine's, a sort of whistling droning sound. It is actually a very relaxing sound. You close your eyes and for a moment imagine the aircraft from the outside. It is flying high, safely and quickly on to the destination. You remember you will be meeting friends when you arrive, it will be great to spend time with friends. You are looking forward to that and telling them about the secret crew rest compartments, but for now you need a good night's sleep. How relaxed you are. You can feel the vibration of the aircraft and along with the relaxing sound of the engines, it makes you feel relaxed.

*** Okay (Childs name) it is time to rest now, and to relax? You know how, your good at relaxing. I think if you were really relaxed, anyone would think you were actually asleep. You may hear some of the sounds in the room, you can hear my voice but it doesn't bother you. You know how to relax, to enjoy the calm and quiet of bed time.

You can hear my voice, but that won't stop you relaxing, it's so easy to relax, to drift down into a restful sleep. You feel sleepy, you may even feel as if your floating, letting go and really relaxing. Your arms and legs may start to feel heavy as you rest and relax.

Your eyes close, because your eyelids have started to feel heavy. Your whole body is starting to relax, to feel loose and heavy. It is a wonderful, warm feeling, to be relaxed, to be comfortable and safe in your bed.

You feel so sleepy, you feel so comfortable and safe. (Childs name), you did so well today, only wonderful dreams will come. We all like to dream nice dreams and to feel safe and comfortable in our bed. You have started to feel that safe, comfortable, relaxed feeling now.

You know a restful night is coming, and you are pleased. That relaxed feeling is now spreading all around your body, from the bottom of your feet all the way up to the top of your head. You feel so very comfortable, relaxed and safe, both inside and outside. All the way through your body, it's a great feeling.

You may still hear the sounds in the room, my voice as I talk. But that doesn't bother you, you don't even notice it any more. You just rest, relax and enjoy that comfortable safe feeling in your bed. Tomorrow is another day, and you will wake up fresh and alert. But for now lets get a good, restful sleep.

***(Feel free to vary and repeat parts as you see fit. Try to use a gentle tone, and don't forget to use the child's name).

❖ ❖ ❖

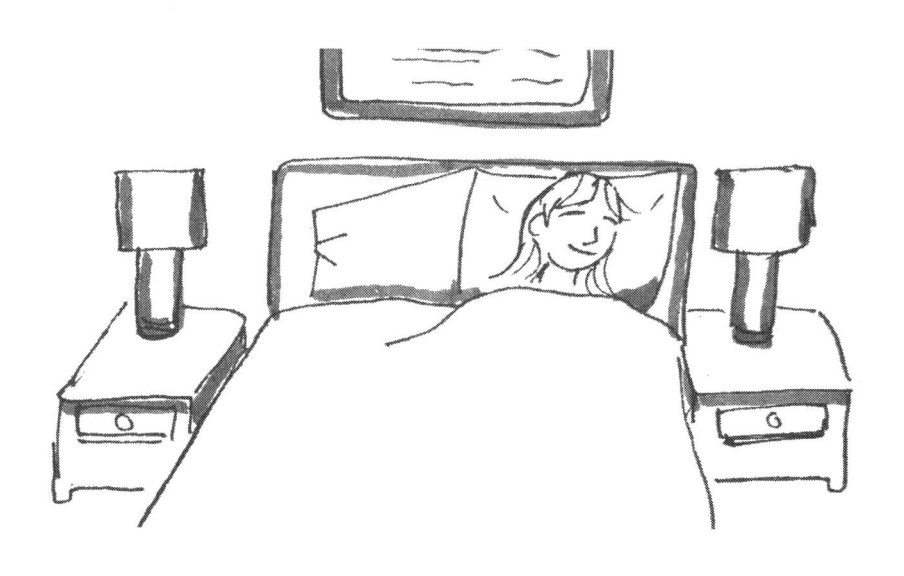

12 - A BIG HOTEL

There are few places quite like a big hotel. A hotel is a place that has rooms for guests. Big, smart and bright. They always seem to be very bright. A big hotel can have hundreds of rooms. They also have different types rooms, from smaller ones for the visitor who is in a hurry and just wants a comfortable bed for the night to huge ones. Those are for holiday makers who want a special treat. The bigger rooms are also popular with famous people, singers and important people.

Each room will of course have beds, and very comfortable ones. The hotel will want every guest to have a good night's sleep. The rooms will have entertainment, in case you need to spend some time in the room. A television, sometimes with a film channel. Also, tea and coffee making with cups and a kettle. Some even have a fridge with drinks inside. There will also be your own bathroom, so you can get nice and clean for dinner. Dinner perhaps in one of the hotels restaurants. Some hotels have restaurants. All different types. In the hotel your room will have a number, so you don't forget which is yours. There have been hotels for hundreds of years. Some were called Inns, and were where your coach might stop for the night. They were very simple compared to hotels today, but you would still get a good meal and a comfortable bed for the night.

The hotel room you're staying in tonight is a very nice one. The first thing you notice when you go in is how clean and tidy it all is. As you walked it you saw a small bathroom to your left. It looked really nice, and had both a bath and shower. You saw a small table with two chairs in front of you, beside a large window. You wondered what you can see from the window, and went to look. It was the sea side. You could see below you the sea front. It was getting dark, but you could clearly see the twinkle of lights being caught on the water further out. It all looked so peaceful and relaxed. Very restful here. Next you saw the bed, it looked really comfortable and relaxing. Your tired, and decided to just lay down for a little. It was then you saw the TV. Your too tired to watch TV, but think maybe you will check it out tomorrow morning.

It's late, and you decided to go to bed for the night. You get changed, and go to brush your teeth. Then, its back to the bed. You climbed in, the sheets were so clean and bright, but a little cold. You pull them up over you and within a minute you start to feel warm and very comfortable. The pillows are just the way you like them, and you shuffle about a little to get really comfortable. You lean over to the light and press the switch, the light goes out. It's very dark but within a couple of minutes your eyes become used to it and you look around the room. You can see the table and chairs. You notice the TV, and try to remember to try it the next morning. You lie back and relax, imagining the sea front and ocean out front. You listen carefully and can hear the waves lapping against the shore, slowly and gently. You can only just about hear it, but it's so relaxing and restful to hear.

** Okay (Childs name) it is time to rest now, and to relax? You know how, your good at relaxing. I think if you were really relaxed, anyone would think you were actually asleep. You may hear some of the sounds in the room, you can hear my voice but it doesn't bother you. You know how to relax, to enjoy the calm and quiet of bed time.

You can hear my voice, but that won't stop you relaxing, it's so easy to relax, to drift down into a restful sleep. You feel sleepy, you may even feel as if your floating, letting go and really relaxing. Your arms and legs may start to feel heavy as you rest and relax.

Your eyes close, because your eyelids have started to feel heavy. Your whole body is starting to relax, to feel loose and heavy. It is a wonderful, warm feeling, to be relaxed, to be comfortable and safe in your bed.

You feel so sleepy, you feel so comfortable and safe. (Childs name), you did so well today, only wonderful dreams will come. We all like to dream nice dreams and to feel safe and comfortable in our bed. You have started to feel that safe, comfortable, relaxed feeling now.

You know a restful night is coming, and you are pleased. That relaxed feeling is now spreading all around your body, from the bottom of your feet all the way up to the top of your head. You feel so very comfortable, relaxed and safe, both inside and outside. All the way through your body, it's a great feeling.

You may still hear the sounds in the room, my voice as I talk. But that doesn't bother you, you don't even notice it any more. You just rest, relax and enjoy that comfortable safe feeling in your bed. Tomorrow is another day, and you will wake up fresh and alert. But for now lets get a good, restful sleep.

*(Feel free to vary and repeat parts as you see fit. Try to use a gentle tone, and don't forget to use the child's name).

◆ ◆ ◆

Printed in Poland
by Amazon Fulfillment
Poland Sp. z o.o., Wrocław